Disney
MINNIE & DAISY
BEST FRIENDS FOREVER

doodle BOOK

Written by: Jessica Ward
Designed by: Steffeni Lum

ISBN 978-1-4231-7410-3
T425-2382-5-13135
Printed in China
First Edition
10 9 8 7 6 5 4 3 2 1
Visit www.disneybooks.com
This book was printed on paper created from a sustainable source.

Disney

Minnie & Daisy

Best Friends Forever

doodle BOOK

Disney PRESS

New York

It's the start of a new school year!

Help Minnie and Daisy **decorate** their lockers.

Daisy's tennis team is getting fresh uniforms. Design something sporty and fun for them to wear.

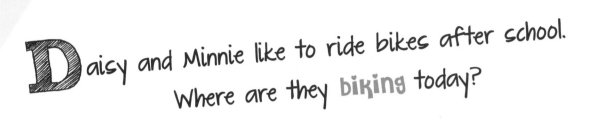

Daisy and Minnie like to ride bikes after school. Where are they **biking** today?

Daisy dreams of **traveling** around the world.
Where will she go first?

It's Daisy's birthday, so Minnie is baking a cake. Help her decorate it!

13

Galloping gooses! Half of Daisy is missing!
Finish **drawing** her.

Minnie just got a Justin Beakber poster to put up in her room. Help her decide where to hang it.

xoxo

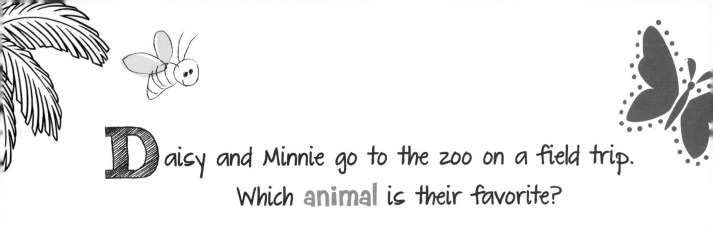

Daisy and Minnie go to the zoo on a field trip.
Which **animal** is their favorite?

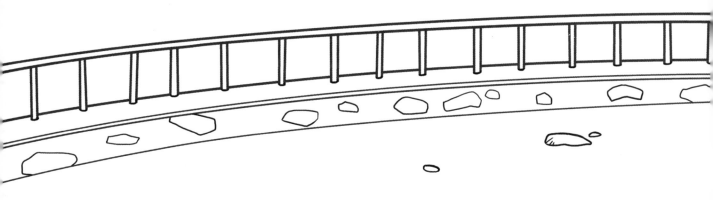

Cowabunga, Daisy!
Finish this gnarly **surfing** scene.

The **homecoming** dance is coming up soon.
What will Minnie wear?

Minnie and Daisy are going to a Halloween party.
Complete their costumes.

coolest

EVER!

On a sunny Saturday afternoon, Minnie and Daisy head to the beach.

Help them build a
super-cool sand castle.

MINNIE

DAISY

BFF

With all her athletic talent, it's a sure thing that Daisy will make the cover of *Sportastic* magazine someday. But which **sport** will she focus on?

Minnie is learning how to play guitar.
Draw her **strumming** a tune.

The fall musical at Mouston Central is *The Wizard of Oz* and the BFFs are starring in it—Minnie as Dorothy and Daisy as Glinda the Good Witch. Complete the dress rehearsal scene.

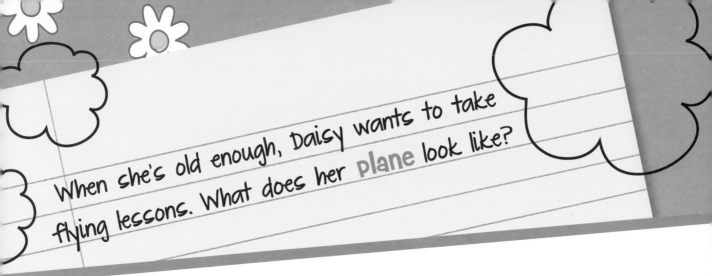

When she's old enough, Daisy wants to take flying lessons. What does her **plane** look like?

If there's one thing Minnie Mouse knows, it's how to accessorize. Add her bow, shoes, jewelry, and more!

Daisy has a secret admirer! What kind of **flowers** does he send her?

Snorkeling shows Minnie a whole
new world under the sea!

It's the most wonderful time of the year.
Help Minnie and Daisy **decorate** the tree.

ORNAMENTS

SWEET!

After acing their biology test, Minnie and Daisy decide to celebrate with an **ice cream sundae**. What's in it?

Minnie dreams of one day winning a Mouscar Award for Best Actress. What gown will she wear to the awards ceremony?

Minnie and Daisy are on a picnic. What did they bring in their **basket**?

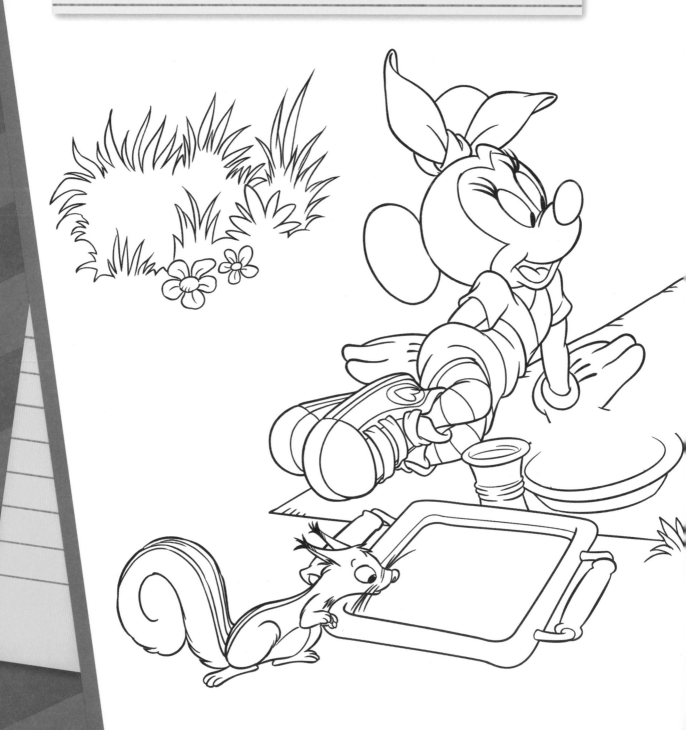

When she's old enough, Daisy wants to drive a totally **sporty car.** What will it look like?

Half of Miss Mouse is missing!
Complete the rest of the drawing.

It's the final inning, there are two outs, and Daisy is at bat. Help her hit a **home run!**

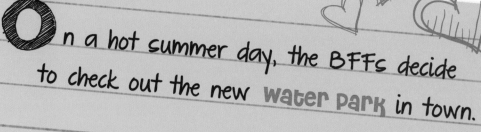

On a hot summer day, the BFFs decide to check out the new water park in town.

Sketch the slippery slide they ride!

Minnie is meeting her big crush after school. What outfit should she choose?

There are very few things that Daisy is scared of, but she has had some nightmares about this **creepy** creature!

It's Turkey Day, and the BFFs are helping their families cook a huge Thanksgiving feast! What did they make?

For the annual school talent show, Daisy auditions with a magic act. What does she pull out of her **hat?**

Polka dots, stripes, flowers, stars . . . Minnie has a bow to go with every outfit. Draw her **favorites!**

Daisy dreams of going on safari in Africa.
What **animals** would she see?

Minnie is writing a screenplay for a movie called Mysterious Mouse: Secret Agent. She plans to direct, produce, and star in the film! Draw the **movie poster.**

MYSTERIOUS MOUSE:

SECRET AGENT

Starring Minnie Mouse

It's a snow day! Help Minnie and Daisy build a cool **snowman!**

There's a big sale coming up at Shoes
Galore, so Minnie is saving her allowance.
What kind of shoes will she buy?

Halloween is just a few days away.
Help Daisy draw a SPOOKY FACE on her pumpkin!

Sometimes Minnie and Daisy like to pretend that they are swashbuckling pirates sailing the high seas! Fill their treasure chest with gold and jewels!

To put the finishing touches on her history report, "Egyptian Mummies," Minnie is designing a colorful **cover.** Help her get an A+!

EGYPTIAN MUMMIES

Daisy knows how much Minnie loves jewelry, so for Minnie's birthday, Daisy is making her a beautiful necklace. What does it look like?

Just in time for spring, Minnie and Daisy are decorating a basketful of eggs. Give them a hand!

Daisy loved pet-sitting for Mrs. Flamingo's sugar glider, so she decides to get a pet of her own.

What type of **animal** does she take home?

Whenever she goes to a carnival, Daisy heads straight for the roller coaster. Now she needs your help to **design** her own!

Minnie likes peppers, mushrooms, and onions;
Daisy likes pepperoni, olives, and pineapple.
Draw their **pizza!**

If Minnie could be on a reality show, it would definitely be *Waltzing with the Stars.* Draw her **dance partner** and decorate her **dress.**

Daisy figures that snowboarding has got to be similar to surfing, so she's getting ready to hit the slopes. What does her snowboard look like?

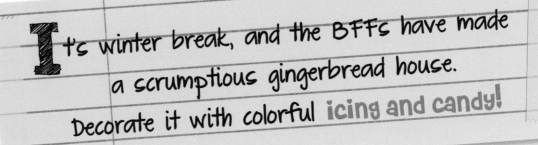

It's winter break, and the BFFs have made a scrumptious gingerbread house. Decorate it with colorful **icing and candy!**

Daisy's favorite clothing store, The Quack, is having a huge sale. Draw the outfit that Daisy is modeling for Minnie in the fitting room.

Last year, Minnie won second prize in the school science fair. This year, she is determined to take first place! What **project** is she working on?

For her history assignment, Daisy is giving a report on mythological creatures. Fill her presentation poster with drawings of a **centaur** (half man, half horse), a **mermaid** (half woman, half fish), and a **griffin** (half eagle, half lion.)

Minnie and Daisy are BFFs—best friends forever.
Draw a picture of yourself with your BFF!

BFF

The new Bryan Gosling movie just came to the theater in Mouston, so of course, Minnie and Daisy were first in line. Which scene is their favorite?

On a rainy day, Minnie and Daisy decide to make friendship bracelets. What do they look like?

Since Minnie loves school dances so much, she volunteers to design the posters for the Spring Formal. The theme is "Disco In FURno: A Tribute to the Seventies." Help her create a **fab flyer**—and don't forget the disco ball!

MOUSTON SPRING FORMAL:

Disco InFURno:
A Tribute to the Seventies

It's a clear, starry night. What do Minnie and Daisy see through the **telescope?**

M innie and Daisy are going to a masquerade party. Draw their **masks!**

After Minnie finishes babysitting for Lilac and Lyle one afternoon, Mrs. Shetland asks Minnie if she will paint a mural in Lilac's room. Minnie knows that Lilac loves unicorns. What does the **mural** look like?

Today's gym class is all about juggling.
What **objects** is Daisy trying to keep in the air?

Minnie just got a new cell phone. Help her **decorate** it!

When Minnie grows up, she hopes to be a famous
fashion designer. Sketch some items from her
first line of clothing!

There's a carnival at Mouston Central this weekend!
Which **ride** are Minnie and Daisy waiting in line for?

Minnie and Daisy both love going to the circus, but the acts they like are very different. Finish the drawing with Minnie's favorite—the acrobats—in one ring, and Daisy's favorite—the lion tamer—in another ring!

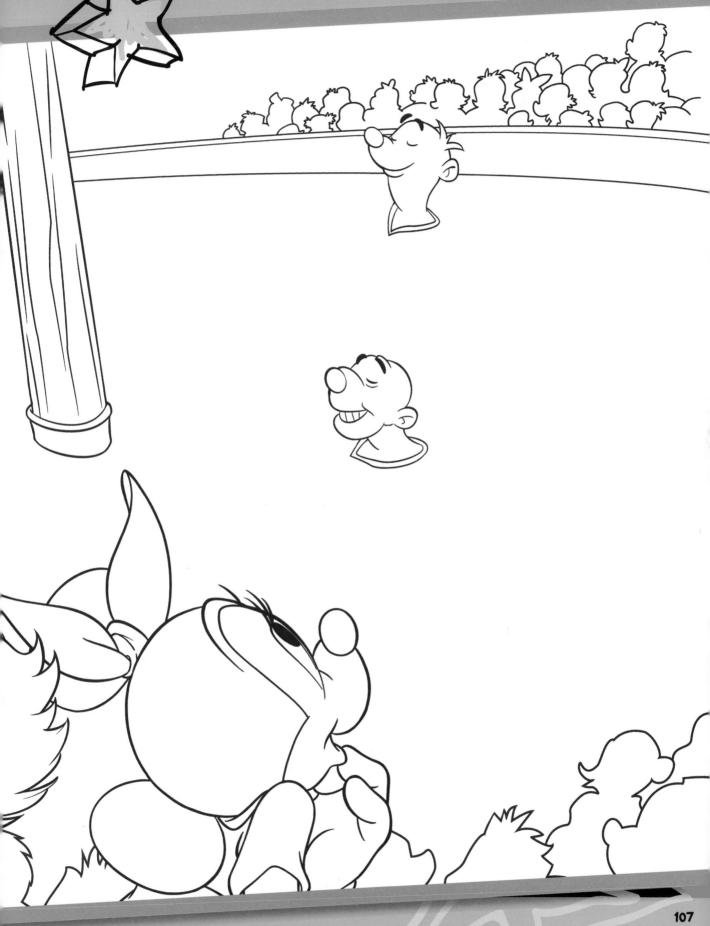

It's been pretty chilly outside lately, so Minnie is knitting something warm and cozy for Daisy. What is she knitting?

Now that Daisy has mastered surfing, she's decided to try windsurfing. Add a colorful **sail** to help her catch the wind!

Minnie and Daisy have matching pins that symbolize their friendship. Design a **pin** for you and your BFF!